Dear Parent:
Your child's love of reading starts here!

Every child learns to read in a different way and at his or her own speed. Some go back and forth between reading levels and read favorite books again and again. Others read through each level in order. You can help your young reader improve and become more confident by encouraging his or her own interests and abilities. From books your child reads with you to the first books he or she reads alone, there are I Can Read Books for every stage of reading:

SHARED READING
Basic language, word repetition, and whimsical illustrations, ideal for sharing with your emergent reader

BEGINNING READING
Short sentences, familiar words, and simple concepts for children eager to read on their own

READING WITH HELP
Engaging stories, longer sentences, and language play for developing readers

READING ALONE
Complex plots, challenging vocabulary, and high-interest topics for the independent reader

ADVANCED READING
Short paragraphs, chapters, and exciting themes for the perfect bridge to chapter books

I Can Read Books have introduced children to the joy of reading since 1957. Featuring award-winning authors and illustrators and a fabulous cast of beloved characters, I Can Read Books set the standard for beginning readers.

A lifetime of discovery begins with the magical words **"I Can Read!"**

Visit www.icanread.com for information
on enriching your child's reading experience.

HarperCollins®, ✆®, and I Can Read Book® are trademarks of HarperCollins Publishers Inc.

Library of Congress Cataloging-in-Publication Data

Hoff, Syd.
  Danny and the dinosaur / by Syd Hoff.
    p.   cm.—(An I can read book)
  Summary: A little boy is surprised and pleased when one of the dinosaurs from the museum agrees to play with him.
  ISBN-10: 0-06-022465-7 (trade bdg.) — ISBN-13: 978-0-06-022465-3 (trade bdg.)
  ISBN-10: 0-06-022466-5 (lib. bdg.) — ISBN-13: 978-0-06-022466-0 (lib. bdg.)
  ISBN-10: 0-06-444002-8 (pbk.) — ISBN-13: 978-0-06-444002-8 (pbk.)
  [1. Dinosaurs—Fiction.] I. Title. II. Series.
PZ7.H672Dan 1993   92-13609
[E]—dc20   CIP
                                                                                                                                        AC

17 18 19 20 LSCC 100 99 98 97 96 95
❖

DANNY AND THE DINOSAUR

Story and Pictures
by Syd Hoff

HarperCollins*Publishers*

One day Danny went

to the museum.

He wanted to see what was inside.

He saw Indians.

He saw bears.

He saw Eskimos.

He saw guns.

He saw swords.

And he saw . . .

DINOSAURS!

Danny loved dinosaurs.

He wished he had one.

"I'm sorry they are not real,"
said Danny.
"It would be nice
to play with a dinosaur."

10

"And I think it would be nice
to play with you,"
said a voice.

"Can you?" said Danny.

"Yes," said the dinosaur.

"Oh, good," said Danny.

"What can we do?"

"I can take you for a ride,"
said the dinosaur.
He put his head down
so Danny could
get on him.

13

"Let's go!" said Danny.

A policeman stared at them.

He had never seen a dinosaur stop

for a red light.

The dinosaur was so tall Danny had
to hold up the ropes for him.

"Look out!" said Danny.

"Bow wow!" said a dog.

"He thinks you are a car," said Danny.

"Go away, dog. We are not a car."

"I can make a noise like a car,"
said the dinosaur.
"Honk! Honk! Honk!"

"What big rocks,"

said the dinosaur.

"They are not rocks," said Danny.

"They are buildings."

"I love to climb,"

said the dinosaur.

"Down, boy!" said Danny.

The dinosaur had to be very careful
not to knock over houses or stores
with his long tail.

Some people were
waiting for a bus.
They rode on the
dinosaur's tail instead.

"All who want
to cross the street
may walk on my back,"
said the dinosaur.

"It's very nice of you to help me
with my bundles," said a lady.

Danny and the dinosaur went
all over town and had lots of fun.
"It's good to take
an hour or two off
after a hundred million years,"
said the dinosaur.

They even looked at

the ball game.

"Hit the ball,"

said Danny.

"Hit a home run,"

said the dinosaur.

"I wish we had a boat,"

said Danny.

"Who needs a boat?

I can swim,"

said the dinosaur.

"Toot, toot!"

went the boats.

"Toot, toot!" went Danny

and the dinosaur.

"Oh, what lovely green grass!"
said the dinosaur.
"I haven't eaten any of that
for a very long time."
"Wait," said Danny.
"See what it says."

PLEASE
KEEP
OFF

30

They both had ice cream instead.

"Let's go to the zoo
and see the animals," said Danny.

Everybody came running

to see the dinosaur.

Nobody stayed to see

the lions.

Nobody stayed to see
the elephants.

Nobody stayed to see

the monkeys.

And nobody stayed to see
the seals,
giraffes or hippos,
either.

"Please go away
so the animals
will get looked at,"
said the zoo man.

"Let's find my friends,"

said Danny.

"Very well,"

said the dinosaur.

"There they are," said Danny.

"Why, it's Danny

riding on a dinosaur,"

said a child.

"Maybe he'll give us a ride."

"May we have a ride?"

asked the children.

"I'd be delighted,"

said the dinosaur.

"Hold on tight," said Danny.

Around and around

the block ran the dinosaur,

faster and faster and faster.

"This is better than
a merry-go-round,"
the children said.

The dinosaur was

out of breath.

"Teach him tricks,"

said the children.

Danny taught the dinosaur
how to shake hands.
"Can you roll over on your back?"
asked the children.

"That's easy,"

said the dinosaur.

"He's smart," said Danny,

patting the dinosaur.

"Let's play hide and seek,"
said the children.
"How do you play it?"
said the dinosaur.
"We hide and you try
to find us," said Danny.

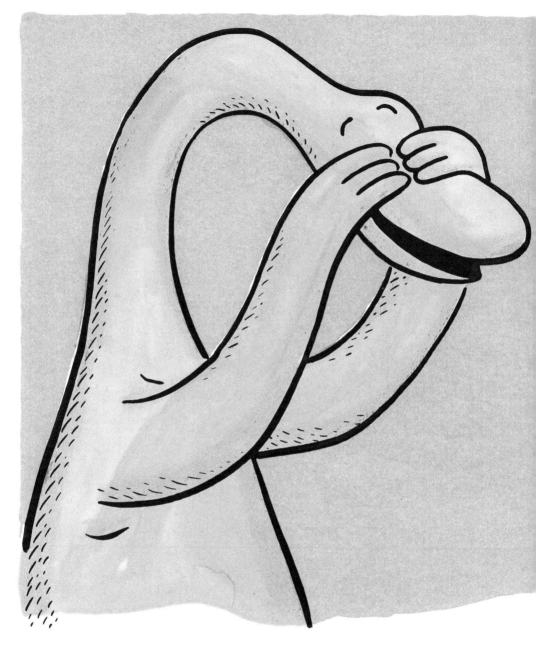

The dinosaur covered

his eyes.

All the children ran
to hide.

The dinosaur

looked and looked

but he couldn't find the children.

"I give up," he said.

Now it was the dinosaur's turn

to hide.

The children covered their eyes.

The dinosaur hid

behind a house.

The children found him.

He hid behind a sign.

The children

found him.

He hid behind a big gas tank.

The children found him.

They found him again

and again and again.

"I guess there's no place

for me to hide,"

said the dinosaur.

"Let's make believe

we can't find him," Danny said.

"Where can he be?

Where, oh, where is that dinosaur?

Where did he go?

We give up," said the children.

"Here I am," said the dinosaur.

"The dinosaur wins,"

said the children.

"We couldn't find him.

He fooled us."

"Hurrah for the dinosaur!"

the children cried.

"Hurray! Hurray!"

It got late and
the other children left.
Danny and the dinosaur
were alone.
"Well, goodbye, Danny,"
said the dinosaur.

"Can't you come

and stay with me?"

said Danny.

"We could have fun."

"No," said the dinosaur.

"I've had a good time—

the best I've had

in a hundred million years.

But now I must get back

to the museum.

They need me there."

"Oh," said Danny.

"Well, goodbye."

Danny watched
until the long tail
was out of sight.

Then he went home alone.

"Oh, well," thought Danny,

"we don't have room

for a pet that size, anyway.

But we did have

a wonderful day."